For Alistair
~J.S.

For Katie
~ C.W.

First published in the United States 1996 by
Little Tiger Press,
12221 West Feerick Street, Wauwatosa, WI 53222
Originally published in Great Britain 1996 by
Magi Publications, London
Text © 1996 Julie Sykes
Illustrations © 1996 Catherine Walters
CIP Data is available.
Printed in Belgium
First American Edition
ISBN 1-888444-01-0
1 3 5 7 9 10 8 6 4 2

Robbie Rabbit
and the
Little Ones

by Julie Sykes

Pictures by Catherine Walters

Little Tiger Press

In a large burrow in Teasel Wood lived
Robbie Rabbit and his family.

One day, Robbie's mother interrupted his
afternoon nap to tell him she was going out.

"Robbie, look after the little ones for me," said Mom.
And before he could say anything, she had hopped
away into the bright sunshine.

Robbie's brothers and sisters were rolling
over each other in the grass.
"All right, little ones," Robbie announced,
"we're going to play a game."

"But we're already playing a game!" cried a little one in surprise.

"I mean a *real* game," said Robbie. "It's called hide-and-seek."

"We don't know how to play it," the little ones exclaimed.

"I'll close my eyes and count to ten while you run and hide. Then I have to find you," Robbie explained. The little ones didn't think it sounded like much fun.

"No wrestling? No kicking or pushing?"

"Of course not!" said Robbie. "Now get ready, and I'll start counting. One, two, three . . . "

By the time Robbie reached ten,
they had all disappeared.

"Ready or not, here I come!" called Robbie,
and he hopped toward the trees.

Sticking out from behind an oak
tree was the tip of a tail.
"A little one!" thought Robbie.
He sneaked over and nipped at it.

"Ouch!" shouted Barney Badger grumpily.
"Go and pull your own tail!"
"Sorry," mumbled Robbie. "I thought
you were a little one."

Robbie scampered to the edge of the woods,
where there were lots of hiding places.
Wait! What was that rustling sound?
Robbie pounced.

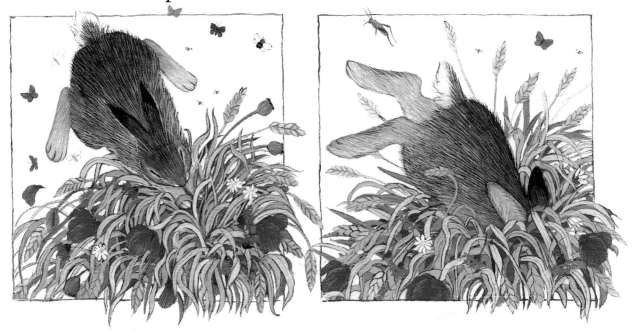

"Eek!" squealed Merry Mouse, and she bit
Robbie on the nose. "You big bully! You've
flattened my nest!"

"I'm sorry," said Robbie. "I was playing a game
with the little ones."

"Well, next time, play somewhere else," snapped
Merry crossly.

Robbie hopped further into the woods.
Near the path was a hollow log.
It appeared to be snoring.
"It *must* be a little one this time," thought Robbie.
"Boo!" he shouted.

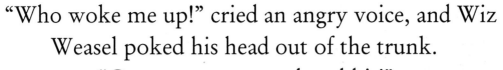

"Who woke me up!" cried an angry voice, and Wiz
Weasel poked his head out of the trunk.
"Go away, you rowdy rabbit!"
"I'm sorry. I thought you were a little
one," said Robbie unhappily.

"This game isn't as much fun as I thought," Robbie
muttered to himself as he bounded along.
"Where *are* the little ones? I hope I haven't lost them."
Suddenly he spotted something hidden in a nearby
bramble bush. Deep in the undergrowth he could see
a speck of fur and a pointed ear.
"A little one!" shouted Robbie, and he tweaked the ear.

"Yap!" a small voice whimpered.
"Grr!" a deeper voice answered, and a fox leapt out
of the bush to defend her cub.
Robbie didn't wait to say sorry this time. He sprang
away as fast as his paws would carry him.

The fox licked her lips as she chased Robbie
through the woods. Just as she was about
to catch him by the tail . . .

. . . Robbie dove into his burrow.
The fox sniffed and snarled,
but the hole was too small for her.

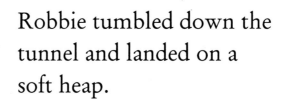

Robbie tumbled down the
tunnel and landed on a
soft heap.

It was the little ones,
all curled up together.

"We've been waiting here forever, Robbie," said one
of them.

"It's a lovely game," said another. "Hiding together
was *such* fun."

"But where have *you* been?" asked a third.

Robbie took a deep breath to tell them about Barney
Badger, Merry Mouse, Wiz Weasel, and the mother
fox, but before he could say anything,
the littlest of the little ones shouted,
"Let's play hide-and-seek again!"